The Usborne
First
Encyclopedia
of
Science

Rachel Firth

Designed by Helen Wood

Illustrated by David Hancock

Edited by Felicity Brooks and Anna Claybourne

Consultants: Sinclair MacLeod and Michael J. Reiss
Managing designer: Mary Cartwright
Digital manipulation: Michael Wheatley

Using Internet links

There are lots of exciting places on the Internet where you can find out about science. This book contains descriptions of Web sites that you can visit by clicking on links on the Usborne Quicklinks Web site. Just go to **www.usborne-quicklinks.com** and enter the keywords "first science". Here are some of the things you can do on the Web sites described in this book:

• Build your own virtual rollercoaster

• Trick your brain with optical illusions

• Learn about the forces in toys

• Find out how to make a magnet maze

Safety on the Internet

Here are a few simple rules to help keep you safe while you are online:

• Ask your parent's or guardian's permission before you connect to the Internet.

• Never give out information about yourself, such as your real name, address or phone number.

• Never arrange to meet someone you started talking to on the Internet.

• If a site asks you to log in or register by typing your name or e-mail address, ask permission from an adult first.

• If you receive an e-mail from someone you don't know, tell an adult. Don't reply to it.

Downloadable pictures

Pictures in this book that have the ★ symbol next to them can be downloaded from Usborne Quicklinks and printed out free of charge, for use in homework or projects. The pictures must not be copied or distributed for any commercial purpose. To find the pictures, go to **www.usborne-quicklinks.com** and follow the simple instructions there.

Site availability

The links in Usborne Quicklinks are regularly updated, but occasionally, you may get a message that a site is unavailable. This might be temporary, so try again later. If any of the sites close down, we will, if possible, replace them with alternatives. You will find an up-to-date list of sites in Usborne Quicklinks.

What you need

Most of the Web sites listed in this book can be accessed using a standard home computer and a Web browser (the software that lets you look at information from the Internet). Some sites need extra programs (plug-ins) to play sound or show videos or animations. If you go to a site and do not have the necessary plug-in, a message will come up on the screen. There is usually a button on the site that you can click on to download the plug-in. Alternatively, go to Usborne Quicklinks and click on **Net Help**. There, you can find links to download plug-ins.

Notes for parents

The Web sites described in this book are regularly reviewed and the links in Usborne Quicklinks are updated. However, the content of a Web site may change at any time and Usborne Publishing is not responsible for the content on any Web site other than its own. We recommend that children are supervised while on the Internet, that they do not use Internet Chat Rooms, and that you use Internet filtering software to block unsuitable material. Please ensure that your children read and follow the safety guidelines printed on the left. For more information, see the **Net Help** area on the Usborne Quicklinks Web site.

A COMPUTER IS NOT ESSENTIAL
TO USE THIS BOOK

This book is a complete, superb, self-contained information book by itself.

Contents

A slug uses its strong stomach muscle to crawl up a plant stem.

What is science?

Science is what we know about the world around us. Why do volcanoes erupt? What is gravity? Is there life on other planets? How do our brains work? Science tries to answer all these questions and many more.

Being a scientist

People who do science are called scientists. They study things by looking at them closely, asking questions, and doing experiments to find out how they work.

Scientists who study animals, such as this macaw, are called zoologists.

Scientists have found out why leaves turn red or brown in the autumn.

Scientists can use their scientific knowledge to help them invent things, like this mobile phone.

SAMSUNG

> **Internet link**
>
> For a link to a Web site where you can find out about some of the useful things scientists have invented, go to **www.usborne-quicklinks.com**

Studies of macaws have shown that their bright feathers may help them to find a mate.

Scientists have found 17 different species (types) of macaws in the wild.

Branches of science

There are hundreds of different kinds, or branches, of science, and many different kinds of scientists. Here are just a few of them.

 ★

Biologists study living things.

 ★

Botanists study just plants.

 ★

Chemists study chemicals.

Technology

Scientists can use their understanding of the world to design or invent new things. Without science, we wouldn't have many of the machines and medicines we have today. Using science in this way is called technology.

Medical scientists use X-ray machines to look inside people's bodies. The picture above is an X-ray photo of a foot. Can you see the bones?

This is a machine called a robot. It can move around and make its own simple decisions.

Some types of robots can do dangerous jobs instead of humans.

What scientists do

To find out about things, scientists do experiments. These are tests that show how living things, objects or substances behave.

Internet link

For a link to a Web site where you'll find lots of fun science experiments to try out, go to **www.usborne-quicklinks.com**

Asking questions

Scientists use experiments to help them answer questions. For example, a scientist might ask, "does music make plants grow faster?"

As an experiment, she could take two groups of plants and play music to just one of them, to see which grew faster.

These pictures show a simple experiment on plants.

A scientist grows two similar groups of plants.

Music is played to only one of the groups.

Later, the two groups can be compared.

Theories

Scientists think up theories that might explain how things work. For example, they might have a theory that penguins travel to a certain area because there is more food there. Then they do experiments to test their theories.

Scientists write down their results and repeat their experiments to make sure they work.

— Transmitter

This penguin is part of an experiment. Scientists have fitted it with a jacket containing a transmitter. (It doesn't hurt the penguin at all.)

The transmitter will send signals that the scientists can collect. From this, they can track the penguin's movements.

Observing

Observing means watching and measuring things very carefully. It's an important part of being a scientist.

Scientists often use tools to help them observe things. For example, astronomers (space scientists) use powerful telescopes to study planets, stars and galaxies.

Telescopes make far away things look nearer. There is a huge telescope in this building that a team of astronomers uses to watch the night sky.

This is a comet. Comets are balls of ice and dust that zoom through space. By observing the path of a comet, astronomers can work out where it will go next.

Do your own experiment

Find out if adding salt to water will make a difference to how things float in it. You will need:
2 half-full glasses of water; 2 fresh eggs; 10 heaped teaspoons of salt

1. Stir the salt into one glass of water until it has dissolved and is invisible.

2. Put an egg in each glass. Do both eggs float? Do they both behave the same way?

You can find out more about floating on pages pages 46-47.

Our Universe

The Universe is the name for space and everything in it, including stars, planets, and our own planet, the Earth. Scientists are always working to find out more about the Universe.

This is the planet Jupiter. It is 11 times wider than the Earth.

Stars and planets

The Universe contains billions of stars. They look small because they are very far away. In fact, each star is a giant ball of burning gas. Some stars have balls of rock, called planets, orbiting (circling) around them.

The Big Dipper   Orion

The patterns stars form in the sky are known as constellations. Here are two of them.

Galaxies

In space, stars and planets form huge groups called galaxies. Our planet, the Earth, and our nearest star, the Sun, are part of a galaxy called the Milky Way.

Although it's just a small part of the Universe, the Milky Way is enormous. The world's fastest plane would take about two million million million years to fly across it.

This is the Milky Way. Scientists think that there are about 200 billion stars in it.

Our Solar System

The Sun is a star. It has nine planets, including Earth, orbiting around it. Together, the Sun and its planets are known as the Solar System.

This picture shows the nine planets in the Solar System, and how big they are compared to each other.

Internet link

For a link to a Web site where you can find out more about the planets in our Solar System and do a quiz about them, go to **www.usborne-quicklinks.com**

Jupiter

Saturn

Neptune   Uranus

Pluto

Mars   Venus

Earth   Mercury

The Earth and Moon

The Earth is the third planet from the Sun. It is the only planet we know where people, animals and plants live.

A smaller ball of rock called the Moon orbits around the Earth. Some other planets have moons too. For example, Saturn has 30.

This is what part of the Earth looks like from space. The blue areas are the seas and oceans.

The red arrows show the path the Moon takes as it orbits around the Earth.

Astronauts (people who travel in space) have visited our Moon six times. This photo shows an astronaut on the Moon.

What is the Earth made of?

Our planet, the Earth, is a huge ball of rock and metal. We live on its crust, or hard surface. Inside, the Earth is so hot that some of the rock and metal there is molten, or melted.

Inside the Earth

Scientists think the Earth is made up of layers, with a round metal core in the middle. In this picture, the Earth has been cut open to show the layers inside.

Crust made of solid rock

Mantle made of partly molten rock

Outer core made of molten metal

Inner core made of solid metal

Earthquakes and volcanoes

The Earth's crust is made up of huge pieces, called plates. They slide around very slowly. When they push against each other, we feel an earthquake. When a volcano erupts, magma, or molten rock, from inside the Earth bursts right out through the crust.

In a volcanic eruption, magma gushes out of the ground. Magma that has come to the Earth's surface is called lava.

Rocks and minerals

The Earth's crust contains many different types of rocks. They are made up of basic ingredients called minerals. Minerals include metals, such as gold and iron, and precious stones such as diamonds.

We use rocks and minerals for all sorts of things.

The salt we put on our food is a kind of mineral.

This building is made from a rock called marble.

Jewellery is often made of metal and precious stones.

This is a slice of a mineral called agate.

Internet link

For a link to a Web site where you can see an animation of a volcano erupting, go to **www.usborne-quicklinks.com**

Watery world

Less than a third of the Earth's surface is land. The rest is covered by seas and oceans. They are home to millions of kinds of fish and other animals.

Coral reefs are underwater structures made by tiny animals called corals. They are home to shellfish, octopuses, sharks and many other fish.

The seasons

In most places on Earth, the year is divided into four seasons. They are spring, summer, autumn and winter.

Changing seasons

The weather changes from season to season. It is coldest in winter and hottest in summer. Many plants also change with the seasons. You can tell what season it is by looking at some kinds of trees.

In the autumn, the leaves on the trees turn red or brown and begin to die.

In the summer, trees like this one are covered in green leaves.

In spring, as it gets warmer, new leaves start to grow on trees.

By winter, all the leaves have died and fallen off.

North and south

The two halves of the Earth are called the northern and southern hemispheres. When countries in the southern hemisphere have their winter, countries in the northern hemisphere have their summer.

The picture on the right shows the Earth's two hemispheres. The dotted line shows the equator. (It's invisible really.)

North Pole

North America

Europe

Northern hemisphere

South America

The equator

Africa

Southern hemisphere

★

South Pole

> **Internet link**
>
> For a link to a Web site where you can watch a cartoon and try a quiz about the seasons, go to **www.usborne-quicklinks.com**

What makes the seasons happen?

The Earth is tilted a little as it goes around the Sun. The hemisphere that is tilted towards the Sun gets more hot sunlight and it is summer there.

The hemisphere tilted away from the Sun has winter. Each year, first one half and then the other is nearer the Sun. This makes the seasons change.

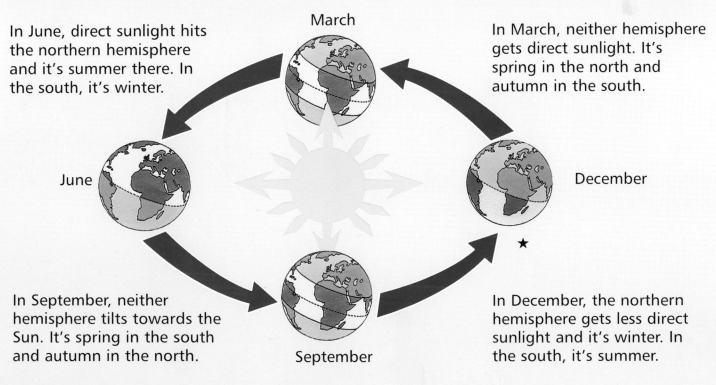

In June, direct sunlight hits the northern hemisphere and it's summer there. In the south, it's winter.

March

June

In September, neither hemisphere tilts towards the Sun. It's spring in the south and autumn in the north.

September

In March, neither hemisphere gets direct sunlight. It's spring in the north and autumn in the south.

December

★

In December, the northern hemisphere gets less direct sunlight and it's winter. In the south, it's summer.

Weather

There are lots of different kinds of weather. It can be rainy, snowy, sunny or windy. The three main things that make the weather happen are the Sun, the air and water.

The Sun gives out heat.

The air moves to make wind.

Water makes rain and snow.

4. The water droplets bump into other droplets and join together to make clouds.

Rainy days

3. Up in the sky, it's cooler and the gas turns back into tiny water droplets.

5. As more water is added, the droplets get bigger and heavier and fall as rain.

The amount of water in the world is always the same. Rain isn't new water. Follow the numbers to find out where rain comes from.

2. The water turns into water vapour, a gas which we can't see, and rises up into the sky.

6. The rain falls down to the ground where it flows back into seas, lakes and rivers.

1. The Sun heats up the water in seas, lakes, rivers, and snow on mountain tops.

Windy weather

When it's windy, it's because the air is moving around. You can't see the wind, but you can see it blowing leaves around and feel it on your face.

A gentle wind is called a breeze. It can help dry wet clothes.

Gales are much stronger winds. They can blow tiles off roofs.

Hurricanes are very strong winds that can do a lot of damage.

Rainbows

Sometimes it rains even though the Sun is shining. Raindrops split sunlight into different colours. When this happens you might see a rainbow. From the ground, it usually looks like an arch, but from an aircraft, it may be a circle.

Make a rainbow

You can make your own rainbow even when it's not raining, as long as the Sun is shining. You will need:
a plastic tray or bowl; a piece of paper; a mirror

1. Put the tray of water in a sunny place, such as on a windowsill, or outside.

2. Stand the mirror in the tray so the Sun can shine through the water onto the mirror.

3. Hold the paper above the tray. Tilt the mirror until you see a rainbow on the paper.

Icy snowflakes

Snowflakes are made when it gets so cold that the water in a cloud freezes and turns into ice. Snowflakes all have six sides or points, but they form millions of different patterns.

Every snowflake is a different shape.

Internet link

For a link to a Web site where you can find out more about hurricanes and watch video clips of them, go to **www.usborne-quicklinks.com**

15

Living things

There are millions of living things on planet Earth. These include plants, animals and people. All living things share certain features.

Living things need a gas called oxygen. A fish gets oxygen from the water it takes in through its mouth.

Air and food

To stay alive, most living things need a gas called oxygen. They also need food. Plants make their own food using energy from the Sun. Animals get energy by eating plants or other animals.

A buttercup plant uses energy from sunlight to grow.

A snail gets its energy from eating the buttercup.

A thrush eats the snail, and gains its energy.

New life and growth

Living things can make new living things. These live on after their parents have died. Animals make babies, and plants produce new plants. As they get older, most living things grow and change.

These baby penguins look like small versions of their parents.

Some animals give birth to live babies. Penguins, like other birds, lay eggs with the babies inside.

Internet link

For a link to a Web site where you can find out about all the different types of living things, go to **www.usborne-quicklinks.com**

Moving

All living things can move. Most animals can move from one place to another. Plants can only move parts of themselves, and they usually move too slowly for you to see.

Some animals, such as this cheetah, can move at very high speeds.

Sensitivity

Living things are sensitive to changes in the world around them, such as changes of light or heat. Animals usually react to these changes more quickly than plants.

A sunflower slowly turns so the flower always faces the Sun.

When a fly touches sensitive hairs on the leaves of a Venus flytrap, the leaves snap shut and trap the fly.

Waste

Plants and animals produce stuff inside them that they don't need. They all have ways of getting rid of the waste.

Dung beetles eat the solid waste (dung) of other animals.

— Fly

Venus flytrap

Cells

All living things are made up of tiny units called cells. Most cells are much too small to see. Scientists have to look at them through microscopes.

This picture shows human fat seen through a microscope. You can see how it is made up of cells.

What is a cell?

A cell is a tiny structure with its own protective skin. Inside, a cell has even smaller parts called organelles.

In many living things, such as humans, millions of cells stick together to make body parts such as bone, skin and muscle.

Plant or animal?

Animal cells have a skin called a cell membrane. Inside, the parts of the cell float in a watery jelly. Plant cells have a cell membrane and a tough cell wall that gives them a fixed shape.

Both plant and animal cells have a nucleus, which controls the cell.

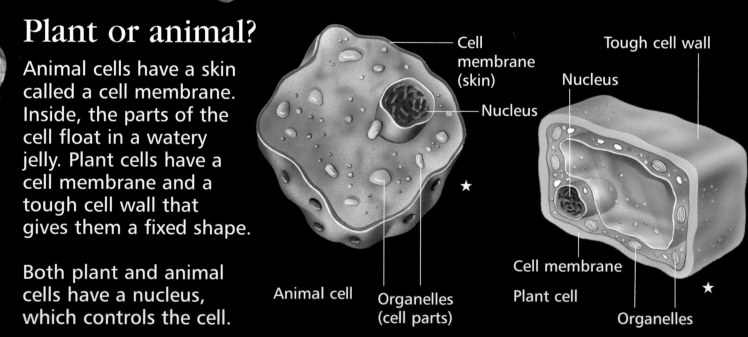

Cell membrane (skin)

Nucleus

Tough cell wall

Nucleus

Cell membrane

Animal cell

Organelles (cell parts)

Plant cell

Organelles

Single-celled creatures

Some very small living things have only one cell. For example, there are single-celled animals called amoebas, and single-celled plants called algae.

Bacteria also have only one cell each. They are not plants or animals, but belong in a group of their own.

Tiny bacteria are all around us, but they are too small to see. Here you can see what salmonella bacteria look like under a microscope.

Internet link

For a link to a Web site where you can find out about some of the bacteria and other tiny living things all around us, go to
www.usborne-quicklinks.com

Looking at cells

Microscopes magnify things, making them look much bigger. When microscopes were invented, over 300 years ago, scientists could begin to look very closely at living things, and cells were discovered.

Scientists use powerful electron microscopes like this to look deep inside cells.

Plants

Plants are living things that can make their own food using energy from the Sun. Scientists have found more than 250,000 species, or types, of plants.

How plants make food

Plants make food inside their leaves. To do this, they mix water from the soil with a gas from the air called carbon dioxide.

To turn these things into food, plants use light energy from the Sun. This process is called photosynthesis (say "foe-toe-*sin*-thuh-sis").

Roots in the soil

Most plants have roots. Roots reach into the soil, holding the plant in place. They also suck up water and chemicals. Plants need water to make food and to keep their cells healthy.

 ★ Without enough water, most plants quickly droop.

 ★ They will recover if they are watered soon enough.

Sun

Plants need light to help them make food and stay alive.

Photosynthesis happens in cells inside a plant's leaves.

Most plants have a central stem.

Roots branch out into the soil to reach as much water as possible.

Plants and seeds

Like all living things, plants reproduce, or have babies. To do this, they make seeds that can grow into new plants. The flower is the part of a plant that makes seeds.

Internet link

For a link to a Web site where you can go on an adventure to solve the mysteries of how plants work, go to **www.usborne-quicklinks.com**

Poppy seedhead

★ When the petals drop off the flower, seeds are released from the seedhead.

★ Some types of seeds, such as dandelion seeds, are blown away on the wind.

★ Other types of seeds are eaten by animals and dropped far away in their droppings.

★ If a seed lands in soil, with enough water and sunshine, it can grow into a new plant.

Plant protection

Most plants stay in one place, so they're in danger of being eaten by animals. To protect themselves, many plants have sharp thorns, stinging hairs or poisonous leaves or berries.

This cactus's thorns protect it from most types of animals.

Grow your own bean plant

You will need:

a glass jar; paper towels; kidney beans; a pot; some compost or soil

1. Line a glass jar with paper towels and keep them damp with water.

2. Put dried kidney beans (a type of seed) between the glass and the paper.

3. Each day look for shoots growing up and little roots growing down.

4. To grow the plants further, plant each bean in a pot of compost and water it.

Animals

Animals are the biggest group of living things. They live all over our planet. Humans are animals too.

Finding food

Unlike plants, animals can move around to look for food. Animals that eat plants are called herbivores. Animals that hunt and eat other animals are called carnivores.

Squirrels are herbivores. They eat nuts.

Chameleons are carnivores. They catch flies.

Badgers eat both plants and animals.

This bald eagle has caught a fish to eat.

Having babies

Most animals can have babies. The babies grow inside their mother's body or inside an egg she has laid.

When babies are big enough, they are born or hatch out of their eggs. This is a crocodile hatching.

Did you know?

• More than a million different species, or types, of animals have been found so far.

• The biggest animal, the blue whale, can be 33m (100ft) long – as long as 3 buses.

• A quarter of all types of animals are beetles.

• A female turbot (a type of fish) can lay up to 14 million eggs at once.

Animal homes

The places where animals and plants live are called habitats. Over time, different species slowly change, or adapt, to suit their habitats.

Safe places

Many animal species are in danger of dying out. This can happen if we destroy wild habitats to make space for farms and towns. Reserves are places where habitats are protected, and animals can live safely.

These animals live in North America, in a hot, wet habitat called a swamp.

Woodpeckers live in woods. They eat insects that live in bark.

Zebra butterflies get their food from flowers.

Green tree frogs have suckers on their feet to climb slippery branches.

Otters are equally at home on dry land or in water.

Cottonmouth snakes live in places where there is long grass. They are also good swimmers.

Terrapins swim under water, but come to the surface to breathe.

Gambusia fish eat mosquito eggs that float on the water surface.

Alligators spend a lot of time in water, where they hunt fish and other animals.

23

Your body

Have you ever wondered what's inside you? Your body is made up of lots of separate parts. They all do different jobs to help you stay alive.

Organs

Organs are important body parts such as your heart, lungs, stomach and brain. Most of them are in your upper body and your head. You can see some of the body's main organs in this picture.

Each organ has a special job to do. For example, your stomach holds the food you eat, and your lungs take air into your body.

How much air can your lungs hold?

You will need:

a plastic bottle; a bendy straw; a bowl of water

 1. Fill the bottle with water and put the lid on. Hold it upside down in the bowl and take the lid off.

 2. Push the straw into the neck of the bottle. Breathe in deeply, then blow gently into the straw until your lungs are empty.

 3. All the air you breathe out will be trapped at the top of the bottle. This is how much air your lungs can hold.

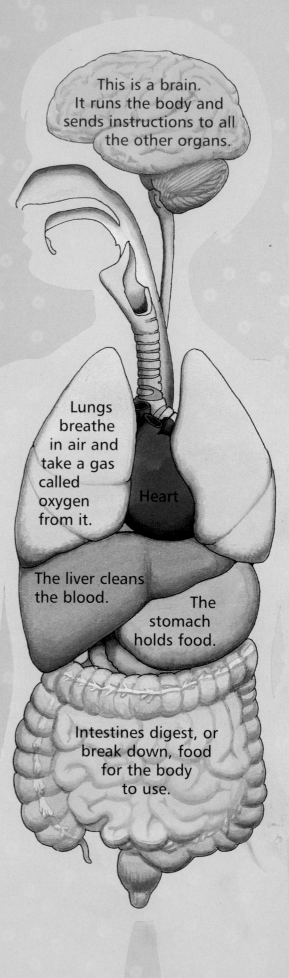

This is a brain. It runs the body and sends instructions to all the other organs.

Lungs breathe in air and take a gas called oxygen from it.

Heart

The liver cleans the blood.

The stomach holds food.

Intestines digest, or break down, food for the body to use.

Blood

As well as organs, a human body contains up to five litres (nine pints) of blood. Your heart pumps blood around your body along thousands of tubes called blood vessels. As it flows along, blood delivers oxygen and food to every part of your body.

Blood is made of cells (see page 18) floating in a liquid called plasma. These pictures show different types of blood cells.

Platelet (part of a blood cell)

White blood cell

Red blood cell

Feel your pulse

To feel your blood being pumped around your body, press two fingers on the inside of your wrist. The beating you can feel is called your pulse.

★

Internet link

For a link to a Web site where you can discover some amazing heart and lung facts and see short movies of blood flowing around your body, go to **www.usborne-quicklinks.com**

Safe in your skin

Your skin gives your whole body a waterproof covering, and protects your insides from dirt and germs. Skin is made up of two main layers.

This close-up photo shows the different layers of some human skin.

Hair

The top layer of skin is called the epidermis.

Underneath the epidermis is a thicker layer called the dermis.

Hair shaft

Hair follicle

Hair root

In some places, the epidermis reaches deep into the dermis and forms a hair follicle. A hair can grow out of each follicle.

25

Bones and muscles

Bones and muscles are your body's support system. They hold you up and let you move around. Without them, you'd be nothing but a helpless blob.

Your skeleton

Together, your bones make up your skeleton, which acts as a framework for your whole body. Bendy joints where bones meet let you move into different positions.

Bones protect your insides too. For example, rib bones in your chest stop the organs inside from getting squashed.

This shows an adult human skeleton with some of its main bones and joints named.

★ Skull

Jaw bone

Collar bone

Shoulder blade

Breast bone

Ribs

Vertebrae (back bones)

Elbow joint

Wrist bones

Pelvis

Hip joint

Finger bones

Coccyx (tail bone)

Femur (thigh bone)

Knee joint

Fibula

Lungs

Heart ★

Tibia (shin bone)

Patella (kneecap)

Foot bones

Ankle joint

Soft skeletons

A baby's bones are partly made of a bendy material called cartilage. As the baby grows, most of the cartilage slowly changes into hard bone.

This is an X-ray picture of a newborn baby's skull. As the baby grows older, the gaps in its skull will slowly close up and the skull will get harder.

Muscles

The bones of your skeleton are moved by muscles. These help you move in all kinds of ways, from walking or swimming to playing the recorder or using a computer.

You also have other muscles (in your heart, for example) that work without you even thinking about them.

There are over 600 muscles in the human body. This picture shows some of the main ones.

Trapezius

Triceps

Deltoid

Biceps

Gluteus maximus

Rectus abdominis

Quadriceps

Gastrocnemius

Gracilis

Internet link

For a link to a Web site where you can watch a cartoon and do a quiz about muscles, go to **www.usborne-quicklinks.com**

Moving muscles

Muscles work by contracting (getting shorter). As a muscle contracts, it pulls on the bones it's joined to, and they move. These little pictures show how muscles contract to bend and straighten your arm.

Biceps

★

Triceps

Biceps

Triceps

★

To bend your arm, the biceps muscle contracts, pulling up the lower arm.

To straighten your arm, the triceps muscle contracts, pulling the lower arm down.

27

What happens to food?

The food you eat gives you the energy you need to live. But to get this energy, you have to turn food into chemicals in your body. This is called digestion.

Your food's journey

As food travels into and through your body, it gets broken down into smaller and smaller bits. Follow the steps on the big picture to find out how this happens.

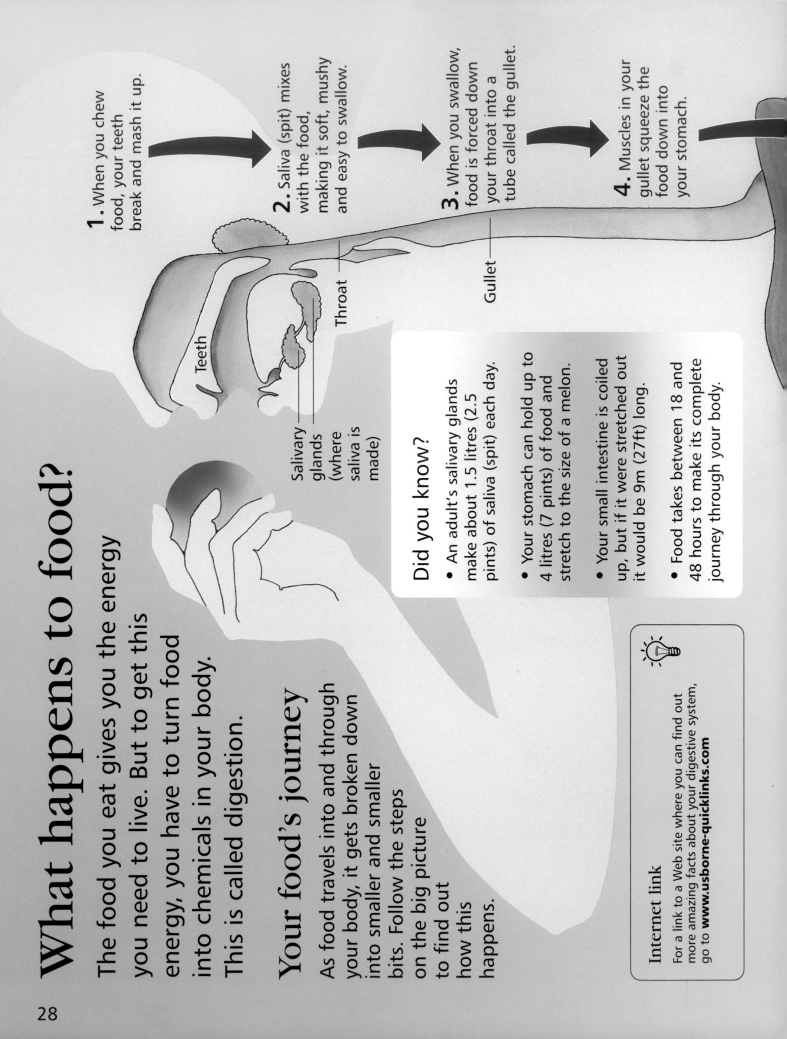

1. When you chew food, your teeth break and mash it up.

2. Saliva (spit) mixes with the food, making it soft, mushy and easy to swallow.

3. When you swallow, food is forced down your throat into a tube called the gullet.

4. Muscles in your gullet squeeze the food down into your stomach.

Teeth

Salivary glands (where saliva is made)

Throat

Gullet

Did you know?

• An adult's salivary glands make about 1.5 litres (2.5 pints) of saliva (spit) each day.

• Your stomach can hold up to 4 litres (7 pints) of food and stretch to the size of a melon.

• Your small intestine is coiled up, but if it were stretched out it would be 9m (27ft) long.

• Food takes between 18 and 48 hours to make its complete journey through your body.

Internet link

For a link to a Web site where you can find out more amazing facts about your digestive system, go to **www.usborne-quicklinks.com**

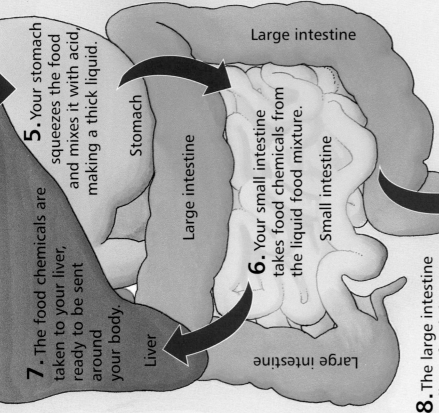

5. Your stomach squeezes the food and mixes it with acid, making a thick liquid.

7. The food chemicals are taken to your liver, ready to be sent around your body.

6. Your small intestine takes food chemicals from the liquid food mixture.

8. The large intestine collects food that can't be digested. It takes water out of it, leaving lumps of waste called faeces.

9. The lumps of waste from your large intestine are squeezed out of your rectum when you go to the toilet.

Large intestine

Stomach

Large intestine

Liver

Small intestine

Large intestine

Rectum

Small intestine

Food for your cells

After food has been turned into chemicals, it is carried all around your body in your blood. Some food is used to give your cells the energy they need to work – for example, to make muscles move. Some food is used to build new cells and repair injuries.

If you eat more food than you need, your body stores it as fat. This is why you get fatter if you eat a lot and don't exercise much.

Waste

Most food contains bits that can't be digested, such as pips and fruit skin. They go into your large intestine and collect into lumps, which end up in the toilet.

Millions of tiny bacteria, like these E. coli bacteria, live inside your intestines. They help themselves to your food, but are usually harmless.

Your brain and senses

Your brain controls your body. Your five senses – sight, hearing, touch, taste and smell – tell your brain what's going on around you, so it can make decisions.

Internet link

For a link to a Web site where you can fool your brain with a selection of optical illusions, go to
www.usborne-quicklinks.com

Brain bundle

Your brain is made of a big bundle of cells called neurons. When you think, your neurons are passing signals to each other. Neurons also link your brain to your sense organs and to other parts of your body.

This picture shows how signals (in green) jump between two neurons in your brain. (They are invisible really.)

Skull

This scan of a person's head shows the brain inside the skull

Seeing things

You see things because light bounces off them and goes into your eyes. Your eyes collect the light patterns and turn them into signals your brain can understand.

1. Light bounces off an object.

4. The optic nerve (made of neurons) carries signals to your brain.

2. The light enters your pupil which is the black dot in the middle of your eye.

3. Patterns of light hit your retina, a patch of special light-sensitive cells on the inside of your eye.

How you hear

Sounds make molecules (tiny particles) in the air vibrate (move back and forth). You hear when these vibrating molecules hit your ears. The vibrations go into your head, and are turned into signals that are sent to your brain.

3. The inner parts of your ear read the vibrations and send signals to your brain.

1. Sounds make vibrations travel through the air.

2. The vibrating air hits a special patch of skin called the eardrum.

The brain is this pale blue and yellow area. The pale yellow lines are folds in the brain's surface.

The brain stem links your brain to your spinal cord and so to the rest of your body.

Brain stem

Taste and smell

Sensitive spots called taste buds on your tongue can detect a few simple tastes.

Sensitive cells in your nose detect different smells, and also help you tell the difference between different flavours.

Tiny pink bumps on your tongue have taste buds in them. The bumps are easier to see after a drink of milk.

Touch

There are millions of sensitive nerve endings in your skin. They can feel heat, cold, pressure and pain. From them, signals zoom along neurons to your brain.

Fingertips have lots of nerve endings. Some blind people can use their fingertips to read Braille writing, which is made up of tiny bumps.

31

Atoms and molecules

Everything is made out of tiny particles called atoms. Atoms can join together in groups called molecules.

Internet link

For a link to a Web site where you can see 3D animated models of lots of molecules, go to **www.usborne-quicklinks.com**

What is an atom?

An atom is like a tiny ball. It has a centre, or nucleus, and outer layers called shells. There are about 100 types of atoms.

Atoms are so tiny that you can't see them. A piece of paper, such as this page, is about a million atoms thick.

Shells

Nucleus

Atoms are made up of even smaller particles. You can see some of them in the nucleus of the atom above.

In atom diagrams, different colours are used to show different types of atoms.

Hydrogen atom

Iron atom

Gold atom

Oxygen atom

Making molecules

Atoms sometimes join together to make bigger units called molecules. This joining together is called bonding.

These pictures show two types of atoms bonding to make water molecules.

Did you know?

• Most of an atom is empty space.

• Some types of atoms, such as francium, do not exist naturally. They can only be made by scientists in a science lab.

• Atoms constantly move around, even in solids. They jiggle, vibrate and bump into each other.

Hydrogen atoms

Oxygen atoms

Water molecules

Water

Water is made up of lots of water molecules.

Materials

All the things around us – rocks, air, water, sand, glass, wood, plastic, and even our bodies – are made of atoms and molecules. Scientists call all these different types of stuff "materials".

 + =

Sodium atoms   Chlorine atoms   Table salt molecules

 + =

Hydrogen atoms   Carbon atoms   Methane gas molecules

Molecules are often shown as balls (the atoms) and sticks (the bonds between them). This shows parts of two molecules of aspirin.

Materials hunt

Can you find things made of these materials in your home or classroom?

★ Paper   ★ China

★ Plastic   ★ Wood

★ Glass   ★ Metal

Chemists mix materials together in glass beakers and flasks like these.

Chemistry

Different materials behave in different ways. For example, if you heat butter, it melts, but if you heat an egg, it gets harder. Salt dissolves quickly in water, but sand doesn't.

Scientists called chemists study how materials behave, change, and bond together. This kind of science is called chemistry.

Solids, liquids and gases

Most materials can exist in three different forms: solids, liquids and gases. In solids, molecules are packed together. In liquids and gases, they're more spread out.

Internet link

For a link to a Web site where you can find more examples of solids, liquids and gases, go to **www.usborne-quicklinks.com**

Gold is a solid.

Solids

The molecules in solids are firmly attached to each other and don't move around much. Because of this, most solids stay the same shape.

Molecules in solids are squashed tightly together.

Liquids

The molecules in liquids are not so squashed together. They can move around more and are not as firmly fixed to each other. This is why liquids can flow, splash and be poured.

Drinks are liquids. They flow into every part of a container.

Molecules in liquids are not squashed together.

Gases

The molecules in gases are not attached to each other at all and move around all the time at high speed. This means that gases quickly spread out to fill the space they are in. They have no shape of their own.

Many gases are invisible. You can only see this gas because it is burning.

Gas molecules don't stick to each other at all.

Make a gas

You can make carbon dioxide gas and blow up a balloon with it. You will need:

a narrow-necked jar; some baking soda; some vinegar; a balloon; a teaspoon

1. Fill a quarter of the jar with vinegar. Put the soda into the balloon, using the teaspoon. ★

2. Stretch the neck of the balloon over the top of the jar. Don't let any soda spill into the jar. ★

3. Quickly lift the balloon up to tip all of the soda into the jar. The vinegar will react with the soda, making bubbles. ★

When the vinegar and soda react (see page 37), they make carbon dioxide gas which fills the balloon, blowing it up a little.

Three forms

The same material can exist as a solid, a liquid or a gas. For example, water exists as a liquid, as solid ice, and as a gas called water vapour.

There is water vapour (water gas) in the air. As it cools, it forms clouds and may turn into rain.

Ice is frozen water. It is a solid.

Water in rivers and seas is a liquid.

How materials change

Materials can change all the time. They can grow, shrink and change between a solid, a liquid and a gas. They can also combine to make new materials.

Changing state

Materials can change between solid and liquid, or between liquid and gas. These changes are called changes of state. They often happen when materials heat up or cool down.

 ★ When juice gets very cold, it turns from a liquid to a solid. This is called freezing.

★ Wax turns from a solid into a liquid as a candle burns. This is called melting.

 ★ When you heat water, it turns from a liquid into a gas. This is called boiling.

 ★ When water vapour cools, it turns into a liquid – rain. This is called condensing.

Inside a freezer, it's cold enough for water to freeze into ice.

Getting bigger

Water expands (gets bigger) when it freezes. Most materials, however, shrink as they get colder and expand as they get hotter. For example, a thermometer* contains a liquid that expands as the temperature rises.

A thermometer contains liquid in a narrow tube. (In this photo, the liquid is black.) As the liquid warms up, it gets bigger and fills more of the tube.

Make water get bigger

Here's what you will need:

a plastic bottle (don't use a glass bottle); a piece of foil; a freezer

 1. Fill the bottle to the top with water. Cover the top with the foil.

 2. Stand the bottle upright in the freezer. Leave it there overnight.

 3. The water pushes the foil upwards as it freezes and gets bigger.

*For more about thermometers, see page 43.

Mixing materials

Materials can be mixed together to make new materials. If you mix sand, cement, broken stones and water, you get concrete. Concrete is useful for building, because it is stronger than any of the ingredients by themselves.

Internet link

For a link to a Web site where you can find out how to make your own simple chemical reaction, go to **www.usborne-quicklinks.com**.

The Catedral Metropolitana in Brazil is made of 16 curved concrete columns.

Reactions

In a mixture, materials are combined but their molecules do not change. Sometimes, however, materials react with each other. This means that when they are mixed, their molecules change and they turn into different materials.

Rusting happens to iron when it is left out in the rain or in damp air.

Molecules of iron react with oxygen atoms and water molecules.

The reaction makes a new type of molecule called iron oxide, or rust.

These rocks formed in Mono Lake in California, USA because of a reaction between two different chemicals in the lake.

Energy

Energy is the power that makes
things happen. You can't see it,
but it's all around you,
making all kinds of
objects move
and work.

Electrical
energy flows
into lights and
changes into
heat and
light energy.

All kinds of energy

Energy comes in many types,
or "forms". For example,
heat, light, electricity and
sound are all forms of energy.

Internet link

For a link to a Web site where you
can find out all kinds of things about
energy, go to **www.usborne-quicklinks.com**

People shouting and
machines moving release
a lot of sound energy.

The same energy

You can't destroy or make energy.
This means the amount of energy
in the Universe is always the same.
But one form of energy can change
into another form.

Plants
change light
energy from
the Sun into
food energy.

Movement energy

Whenever something moves, it has energy. The energy of something that is moving is called kinetic energy.

At the top of the rollercoaster, the car contains stored energy.

To fly, these birds change energy stored in their bodies into kinetic energy.

As the car goes down the hill, stored energy changes into kinetic energy.

These flags have kinetic energy as they flutter in the breeze.

These children have a lot of kinetic energy because they are running fast.

Stored energy

Potential energy is energy that is stored, ready to use. When it's used, it turns into another form of energy, such as kinetic energy or heat.

As the hammer is lifted up, it gains a store of potential energy.

Food turns into stored energy in our bodies. A toffee apple will give this boy enough energy to walk for 20 minutes.

This boy's video camera uses electrical energy that's stored in a battery.

Forces

A force is a push or a pull that makes an object do something. For example, if you kick a ball, the force of your kick makes the ball move. Forces can also make things change their direction, speed and shape.

Direct forces

Some forces work by touching the object they are pushing or pulling on. These are called direct forces. Kicking a ball, lifting a pen or pulling your sock off are all examples of direct forces.

Pushing a toboggan is a direct force.

Pulling a toboggan uphill on a rope is a direct force.

From a distance

Some forces don't have to touch the things they work on. For example, gravity* pulls you down when you jump off a wall. A magnet pulls paperclips towards it. Scientists are still not sure how these distant forces work.

Forces can stop things too. This snowdrift has a force that has stopped this toboggan.

Gravity is a distant force. It is pulling the toboggans downhill, but not touching them.

Internet link

For a link to a Web site where you can find out about the forces in toys, go to **www.usborne-quicklinks.com**

*For more about gravity, see pages 44-45.

Balanced forces

When something isn't moving, you might think that there are no forces working on it. In fact, there are, but they are balanced against each other, and cancel each other out.

These two tug-of-war teams are not moving, because the forces they make are balanced. To win, one of the teams must use more force.

Using forces

We use forces all the time to move things, lift things and travel around. Machines help us to use forces to do things we can't do on our own. They turn our energy, or other forms of energy such as electricity, into the right kinds of force to do different jobs.

A digger turns electrical energy into a pulling force to scoop up a heavy load of soil.

Scissors are simple machines. Their sharp blades use the force of your fingers to cut things.

Hot and cold

Heat is a form of energy. Whenever you heat something up, you are giving it more energy.

Heating up

When many materials heat up, their molecules spread out. This makes them expand, or get bigger. When they cool down, they contract, or get smaller, again. As air heats up, it expands a lot, making it much lighter than cold air. This is why hot air balloons float.

The hot air inside these balloons is lighter than the air they float in. For more about floating, see pages 46-47.

Moving around

Heat moves from hotter to colder places. For example, hot food goes cold because its heat moves into the cooler air around it. You can't usually see heat, but it can be photographed with an infrared camera.

This picture was taken using an infrared camera. The red areas show where the buildings are giving out the most heat.

The Golden
Gate Bridge in
San Francisco, USA

Bridge gaps

Bridges often get slightly
longer as they heat up in the
sun. Large bridges have special
joints with gaps in them, so that
there's room for them to expand.

This is an expansion joint.
Joints like these allow
bridges to expand and
contract. Without them,
bridges could break and
collapse.

★ When a bridge expands in
hot weather, these plates
are pushed together.

— Bridge

Expansion and contraction

You can do an experiment to see
how air expands when it is heated
and contracts when it cools down.
This is what you will need:

a bowl; a bottle; a balloon

1. Ask an adult to hold the
empty bottle under hot water
for a minute. Stretch the
balloon over its neck.

 ★

2. Half-fill the bowl with cold
water and stand the bottle in
it. The air cools and shrinks,
pulling the balloon inside.

 ★

3. Empty the bowl and ask
an adult to add hot water to
it. The expanding warm air
pushes the balloon out again.

 ★

Internet link

For a link to a Web site where you
can watch a cartoon and play a
game about heat, go to
www.usborne-quicklinks.com

Measuring hotness

Temperature means how hot
something is. It is measured in
degrees Centigrade (°C) or
degrees Fahrenheit (°F).
Normal room temperature
is about 20°C (68°F).

Temperature is measured
using a thermometer.
Can you see what the
temperature is on
this thermometer?

★

43

Gravity

When you jump up in the air, you drop back down again. This is because there's an invisible force pulling you down to the ground. This force is called gravity.

Mars

Pulling together

All objects have gravity and make a slight pull on other objects. With small objects, this force is too small to have an effect. But huge objects like planets have enough gravity to pull other things towards them.

Mercury

In empty space, far away from stars, planets and moons, there is hardly any gravity. This is why astronauts float.

Gravity on other planets

The bigger an object is, the stronger its gravity is. Very big planets, like Jupiter, have much stronger gravity than Earth. Small planets and moons have weaker gravity than Earth.

Jupiter's gravity is more than twice as strong as Earth's. If you could visit Jupiter, you wouldn't be able to move because its gravity is so strong.

Jupiter

Jupiter's moon Io is quite small and its gravity is much weaker than the Earth's. You could jump many times higher on Io than you can on Earth.

This is Io, one of Jupiter's many moons.

The Sun

Venus

The Earth is in
orbit around
the Sun.

The Moon is in
orbit around
the Earth.

Testing gravity

Gravity pulls objects at the same speed,
even if they have different weights. Try
testing this yourself. You will need:

tissue paper; a coin; two identical boxes (such as
camera film boxes or food pots with lids)

1. Carefully tear a piece of
tissue paper the same size
as the coin. It will be lighter
than the coin. ★

2. Drop the paper and the
coin from the same height.
The paper falls more slowly
because air gets in its way. ★

3. Now put the coin in one
box and the paper in the
other. Put the lids on and
drop both boxes together. ★

4. The boxes have the same
air resistance and land at the
same time, even though they
are different weights. ★

Internet link

For a link to a Web site where you
can find out how much you would
weigh on planets which have more
or less gravity than Earth, go to
www.usborne-quicklinks.com

In orbit

In space, large objects orbit,
or travel around, each other.
Planets orbit the Sun. Moons
orbit planets. This happens
because of gravity.

Gravity doesn't pull planets
and moons right together,
because they're moving too
fast. This diagram shows
how orbits work.

Moon

Planet

Moons move very fast.
A moon is always trying
to fly away from its
planet in a straight line.

Meanwhile, the planet's
gravity pulls the moon
towards it. The two forces
balance out and the moon
circles around the planet.

Floating

If you throw a stone into a pond, it will sink to the bottom. But if you put a balloon in some water, it will float. Why do some things float and others sink?

Weight and size

Floating is all about density – how heavy something is for its size. For example, a cork is light for its size. A piece of iron the same size as a cork is much heavier, because iron is denser than cork. Objects that are denser than water sink in water. Objects that are less dense than water float in water.

Internet link

For a link to a Web site where you can find out how to make a raisin float and sink in a fizzy drink, go to **www.usborne-quicklinks.com**

These inflatable rings are light for their size and float well.

If you try to push an inflatable ring under water, you'll feel the water pushing back.

Upthrust

Things float because water pushes up on them more than they push down. This upward force is called upthrust. If an object is denser than water, the water cannot provide enough upthrust, so the object sinks.

Does it float?

Guess which things will float in water and then see if you were right. You will need:

a bowl of water; solid things, such as a cork, a candle, a coin, an apple, a raisin, a plastic toy, an eraser.

1. Make a chart to compare your guesses with what actually happens.

2. Try floating different objects and write down which of them really float.

	Will it float?	
	Guess	Actual
Cork	✓	
Coin	✓	
Candle	✗	
Apple	✗	

How do ships float?

Some ships are so huge, it seems amazing that they float – but they do. Even if a ship is made of heavy iron, it has a lot of air inside it. This makes the ship less dense than water, so it floats.

This big cruise ship is light for its size because it has lots of air inside it.

This floating red buoy is used to warn boats that this stretch of water is dangerous.

Floating in air

Floating in air is just like floating in water. Anything that is less dense than air will float in it. But because air is very light itself, not many other things are light enough to float in it.

People are almost the same density as water, and only just float. Air-filled life belts can help people to float better.

These balloons are filled with a gas that's less dense than air. It makes them float.

Salty sea

Salty water is denser than pure water. This makes it easier for people to float in it. A lake in Israel called the Dead Sea has water that's so salty, it's very easy to float in.

This woman is floating in the very salty water of the Dead Sea.

Friction

Whenever an object tries to slide across a surface, it is slowed down by the two surfaces gripping each other. This force is called friction.

Internet link

For a link to a Web site where you can set the friction, speed and shape of a rollercoaster ride, go to
www.usborne-quicklinks.com

The rough...

Friction slows things down because objects have rough surfaces. The rougher the surface, the more friction there is, and the more the object slows down.

This snowboarder can move very fast because there's not much friction between the smooth snow and the smooth snowboard.

...and the smooth

Very smooth surfaces don't have much friction and often feel slippery. If you are on a smooth surface, you can move fast without being slowed down very much.

Getting a grip

As well as slowing down moving things, friction helps things stay still. If it weren't for friction, we wouldn't be able to grip onto anything, or even stand up without slipping.

The soles of walking boots are moulded into rough ridges. This makes lots of friction to stop the walker from slipping.

48

Hot friction

Wherever there is friction, there is heat. This is because as objects rub together, friction turns kinetic, or movement, energy into heat energy. There's more about energy on pages 38-39.

When a Space Shuttle comes back to Earth, it glows red hot because of friction between its surface and the air.

Coin warmer

To see how friction heats things up, try to warm up a metal coin using friction. You will need:

a coin; a pad of paper

1. Hold the coin flat on the paper with one finger on top of it, like this:

2. Press down and rub the coin very fast from side to side about 50 times.

The coin warms up because there is lots of friction between it and the paper. The friction turns the energy of the coin's movement into heat energy.

Streamlining

Even air and water cause friction when things move through them. Cars, planes and boats are built so that water or air can move past them in smooth lines to reduce friction. This is called streamlining.

Dolphins have streamlined bodies which help them to move fast in water.

Magnets

A magnet is a piece of metal that can pull some other types of metal towards it. Magnetism is a force. It happens because of the way atoms are arranged inside the metal.

Iron filings (tiny bits of iron) stick to the parts of this horseshoe-shaped magnet where its magnetic force is strongest.

Pushing and pulling

Magnetic forces are strongest at the two ends of a magnet. These ends are called the north pole and the south pole. If you try to put two magnets' poles together, they will either stick to each other or push each other away.

A north pole and a south pole always pull towards each other. This is called magnetic attraction.

Two poles of the same type always push each other away. This is called magnetic repulsion.

Magnetic fields

The area of force around a magnet is called its magnetic field. Our planet is magnetic and has its own magnetic field. It pulls compass needles so that they always point north.

Like all magnets, the Earth has magnetic north and south poles. They are near the North Pole and South Pole you can see on a globe.

Magnetic north pole

Magnetic south pole

Magnets at work

You might use magnets to stick notes on your refrigerator. They are also used inside motors, DVD players and watches. Because magnets only attract some metals, such as iron, they are also used to separate materials from each other.

Which metals?

Try testing different metal things around your house with a magnet. You will need:

a magnet; metal objects, such as pins, coins, scissors, cutlery, jewellery

Will it stick?	Guess	Actual
Tin can	✓	☐
Coin	✓	☐
Bottle	✗	☐
Ball	✗	☐

1. Guess which objects the magnet will attract.

2. Now test them by seeing if the magnet sticks to them.

The objects the magnet sticks to probably contain some iron, steel or nickel.

This huge magnet is being used to separate different types of metal so that they can be re-used.

"Maglev" trains use magnetic repulsion to make them float just above a rail. This allows them to move very smoothly.

Internet link

For a link to a Web site where you can find out how to make a magnet maze, go to **www.usborne-quicklinks.com**

Light and colour

Light is a form of energy. Most of the light on our planet comes from the Sun. Light comes from other places too – electric lights, candle flames and even some types of animals.

Lines and shadows

Light always travels in straight lines. If light hits an object that's not see-through, it can only shine past it, not around it. This makes a shadow where the light can't reach.

★ Light shines in straight lines. Shadows happen because rays of light cannot bend around objects.

Light can turn a corner if it reflects (bounces) off a surface, such as a mirror.

★ You can make light turn a corner. If you shine a lamp or torch at a mirror, the light will bounce off it.

Glow worms can make light as bright as the display lights on a sound system.

The speed of light

When you flick a light switch, light seems to fill the room instantly. This is because light travels very fast. It moves at 300,000km (186,000 miles) per second.

It takes eight minutes for light to travel from the Sun to the Earth.

Internet link

For a link to a Web site where there are activities to help you to find out more about colours, go to **www.usborne-quicklinks.com**

52

Seeing light

We see things because our eyes are designed to collect and sense light (there's more about eyes on page 30). When we see an object, we're really seeing light reflecting off it.

We see the Moon because light from the Sun reflects off it.

Colours

Bright white light is made up of different colours of light mixed together.

We see colours because some objects only reflect one colour of light. For example, a green leaf only reflects green light, so it looks green.

A piece of shaped glass called a prism can split white light into all its colours.

White light shining into prism

Prism

Separate colours of light shining out of prism

Sometimes raindrops act like mini-prisms. They split sunlight into lots of colours, making a rainbow.

Did you know?

• Most people can detect more than 10 million different shades of colour.

• Some people are "colourblind". They can see some colours, but find it hard to tell the difference between red and green.

• Many animals see only in shades of grey, not in colour.

• Scientists think it's impossible for anything in the Universe to travel faster than light.

Sound

Sound is a form of energy. It is made of vibrations (back-and-forth movements) that can move through air, solid things and liquids, but not through empty space.

Sound vibrations

When you hit a drum, speak or clap your hands, molecules in the air vibrate. We hear sounds because the vibrations travel through air, or other substances, and hit our ears. (Read more about ears on page 31.)

The loudest sounds, such as a rocket lift-off (180 decibels), will damage your ears.

A rattlesnake can make a rattling sound with its tail to scare enemies. The movement of rings on its tail makes molecules in the air vibrate.

Loud and soft

The volume (loudness) of a sound depends on how big the vibrations are. Volume is measured in units called decibels. This chart shows how loud different sounds are in decibels.

Rustling leaves 10dB

Whispering 20dB

Talking 50dB

Vacuum cleaner 72dB

Food blender 88dB

Thunder 115dB

Jet plane taking off 130dB

| 0 | 10 | 20 | 30 | 40 | 50 | 60 | 70 | 80 | 90 | 100 | 110 | 120 | 130 | 140 |

dB (decibels)

High and low

Fast sound vibrations make high sounds. Slower sound vibrations make lower sounds. The highness or lowness of a sound is called its pitch. Some animals can hear pitches we can't hear.

Internet link

For a link to a Web site where you can find out how to make a musical instrument and make your own sounds, go to **www.usborne-quicklinks.com**

This farmer's whistle makes a very high sound. Dogs can hear it, but people can't.

Elephants can make sounds so low that people can't hear them.

Scientists know that blue whales make the lowest, loudest sound of any animal.

Making music

Musical instruments have parts that vibrate to make sounds. When someone plays an instrument, they make different notes by changing the speed of the vibrations.

On a violin, shorter strings vibrate faster and make higher-pitched notes. Violin players make the strings shorter or longer with their fingers.

Feel sound vibrations

You can't normally feel sound vibrations in the air, but you can in this experiment. You will need:

a radio; a blown-up balloon

Turn the radio on and hold the balloon next to its speaker. The vibrations travel through the balloon and into your fingers.

Electricity

Electricity is a very useful form of energy. It can easily be changed into other forms of energy, such as light and heat. It makes lights, televisions and computers work. Most of the electricity we use comes from power stations.

Lightning is a kind of static electricity that's made when water molecules inside clouds rub together during storms.

In power stations, machines called generators turn energy from fuel, such as coal or gas, into electricity.

Cables and pylons carry electricity to transformers.

Transformers, like this one, make electricity safe for us to use.

Getting electricity

Electricity travels from power stations to homes along underground cables, or wires attached to high pylons. They are kept out of reach, because if electricity touches you, it can give you a dangerous shock.

Here, the cables go underground.

56

Using electricity

When an appliance, such as a toaster, is plugged in, it is connected to the electricity supply. Electricity flows into it and gives it the energy to work. Plastic does not conduct, or carry, electricity well, so it is used to cover electrical appliances. This stops you from getting a shock.

Can you guess which of these uses the most electricity in one minute?

Answer: the hairdryer

Internet link

For a link to a Web site where you can find out how to make electricity from a lemon, go to **www.usborne-quicklinks.com**

Static electricity

Static electricity is a form of electricity that builds up in some substances when they are rubbed together. It can make objects stick to each other. Do you ever feel a small shock when you touch metal? This is caused by a small build-up of static in your body as you move around.

Make static electricity

You will need:

a balloon; a sweater

1. Blow up a balloon, and rub it up and down on a sweater a few times.

2. Gently put the balloon on the wall. Static electricity makes it stick there.

Transformer

The orange and yellow lines show the route the cables take underground.

Electricity flows from the underground cables into homes.

Computers

Computers are information machines. They can store numbers, words, pictures and other information, and process them, or make changes to them.

How computers work

Computers contain lots of circuits. These are pathways that can carry electricity. Information travels around them very fast as a code made of electrical signals.

Internet link

For a link to a Web site where you can click on the parts inside a computer to find out what they do, go to **www.usborne-quicklinks.com**

Monitor

This is a modern home computer. You enter information using the keyboard and mouse, and it is displayed on the monitor. Information is processed inside the CPU or Central Processing Unit.

Speaker

CPU

Mouse

Keyboard

This picture shows some of the electronic circuits inside a computer.

Scientists often use computers to help them make scientific pictures. This is a computer-generated image of DNA, an important molecule found in living things.

Hardware and software

Computer equipment is called hardware. To work, computers also need instructions called software. Computer programmers make software by writing sets of special instructions, called computer programs.

This picture of a mouse head was made using 3D animation software. Here you can see two of the different stages involved in creating it.

On the Internet

Computers can be linked together, or networked, so that they can share information. The Internet is a huge worldwide network that any computer can be connected to. It has lots of uses.

Information is stored on the Internet in the form of Web pages. Each page is a screen full of text or pictures. Here are some examples*:

Changing the world

Since they were invented in the 1950's, computers have changed the world. They do sums much faster than humans, and make it easy to send information around the world.

Computers have helped scientists to explore space. This computer-controlled robot was sent to Mars to study its surface.

*Microsoft® Internet Explorer, Microsoft® Outlook®

Science words

This page explains some of the words you will find in this book and other science books.

atom one of the very tiny units that everything is made of.

bacteria tiny single-celled creatures.

cartilage a material like bone, but softer and bendier.

cell a very small living unit. All living things are made up of cells.

chemical reaction a change that sometimes happens when two materials are mixed together.

contract get smaller.

density how heavy a material is for its size.

digestion the way your body breaks down food into useful chemicals.

electricity a form of energy which is used to make machines work.

endangered species a type of living thing that's in danger of dying out.

energy the power that makes things work. Heat, light, movement and electricity are all forms of energy.

equator an imaginary line around the middle of the Earth.

expand get bigger.

experiment a scientific test to find out about how something works.

force a push or a pull. Forces can make things move, stop, speed up, slow down or change shape.

friction a force that slows things down as they rub or slide against each other.

galaxy a huge group of stars.

gravity a force that pulls objects towards each other.

habitat the place where an animal or plant lives, such as a wood or a lake.

heat a form of energy which we can feel. It flows from warmer objects into cooler ones.

the Internet a worldwide network of computers that are linked together so that they can share information.

kinetic energy the kind of energy that something has when it moves.

light a form of energy that we can sense with our eyes.

magnet a piece of metal that pulls some types of metal towards it.

materials the different kinds of stuff all around us, such as water, metal, wood, glass and plastic.

Milky Way the name of the galaxy that our planet, the Earth, is part of.

molecules tiny particles made up of atoms. Everything is made of them.

moon a ball of rock that orbits around a planet.

nucleus the central, most important part of a cell or atom.

observe look at something carefully.

orbit travel around a larger object.

organ a body part, such as the heart, lungs, eyes, liver or brain.

particle a very small piece or part.

photosynthesis the way plants make food using energy from the Sun.

pitch how high or low a sound is.

planet a large ball of rock or gas that orbits around a star.

poles the parts of a magnet where its pulling power is strongest.

potential energy energy that's stored up and ready to use.

reproduce make babies. All plants, animals and other living things reproduce.

robot a machine that can make its own decisions.

science what we know about the Universe and how things work.

skeleton a framework of bones that holds you up and protects your insides.

Solar System our Sun and all the planets and moons orbiting it.

species a type of plant, animal or other living thing.

star a huge ball of very hot gas floating in space.

the Sun the star that our planet, the Earth, orbits around.

technology using science to invent machines and other useful things.

temperature how hot something is.

theory an idea about how something works or why it is the way it is.

the Universe everything that exists in space, including our world.

upthrust a pushing force that makes things float.

X-ray a kind of photograph that can show the inside of the body.

Index

Acknowledgements

The publishers are grateful to the following for permission to reproduce material:

Key
t = top, m = middle, b = bottom, l = left, r = right

Cover Digital Vision; John Russell; p1 Digital Vision; p3 Digital Vision; p4tr Digital Vision; p4c Samsung Electronics UK: The Samsung SG-A400 is another example of an innovative product from Samsung Electronics UK; p4bl Jorg & Petra Wegner/Bruce Coleman The Natural World; p5tr Mehau Kulyk/Science Photo Library; p5br Sam Ogden/Science Photo Library; p6 William Curtsinger/Science Photo Library; p7tr RobertHarding.com; p7br Roger Ressmeyer/CORBIS; p8tl Stockbyte; p8br BSIP/CHAIX/Science Photo Library; p9t NASA; p9t Digital Vision; USGS; Digital Vision; p9c Digital Vision; p9bl Stockbyte; p9br Digital Vision; p10bl Digital Vision; p11tr Martin Bond/Science Photo Library; p11br Digital Vision; p12 Richard Hamilton Smith/CORBIS; Digital Vision; p14tl Digital Vision; p14tc Douglas Peebles/CORBIS; p14tr Digital Vision; p16tr Stockbyte; p16b Digital Vision; p17br Kim Taylor/Bruce Coleman The Natural World; p18tl Prof. P. Motta, Dept. of Anatomy, University "La Sapienza", Rome/Science Photo Library; p19tr Dr. Linda Stannard/UCT/Science Photo Library; p19br Colin Cuthbert/Science Photo Library; p21br Danny Lehman/CORBIS; p22tr Natural Selection Inc./Bruce Coleman The Natural World; p22bl Bruce Davidson/NaturePL.com; p25t National Cancer Institute/Science Photo Library; p25b Lester V. Bergman/CORBIS; p26bl Dave Roberts/Science Photo Library; p29bl Juergen Berger, Max-Planck Institute/Science Photo Library; pp30-31c Mehau Kulyk/Science Photo Library; p31br Garry Gay/Alamy.com; p32b Digital Vision; p33tr BSIP, Barthelemy/Science Photo Library; p33br Digital Vision; p34tl Michael Freeman/CORBIS; p34lc Adrienne Hart-Davis/Science Photo Library; p34bl Larry Lee Photography/CORBIS; p35r Digital Vision; p36tr foodfolio/Alamy.com; p36bl Adrienne Hart-Davis/Science Photo Library; p37tl Oscar Niemeyer/www.arcaid.co.uk; p37br Phil Schermeister/CORBIS; p41b Lowell Georgia/CORBIS; p42tr Digital Vision; p42b Alfred Pasieka/Science Photo Library; p43t Dave G. Houser/CORBIS; p44 Courtesy of NASA/JPL/Caltech; p44tr NASA/JPL/Malin Space Science Systems; USGS; p44br Courtesy of NASA/JPL/Caltech; p45 Courtesy of NASA/JPL/Caltech; p45tl NASA; p45ml Digital Vision; Courtesy of NASA/JPL/Caltech; p47 Hugh Sitton/Getty Images; p48c Brian Bailey/CORBIS; p49tr Digital Vision; p49br George D. Lepp/CORBIS; p50tr TEK IMAGE/Science Photo Library; p51tr Alex Bartel/Science Photo Library; p51b Transrapid International; p52cl Bruce Coleman The Natural World; p52br NASA; Digital Vision; p53tl Digital Vision; p53rc Phototake/Robert Harding Picture Library; p53br Digital Vision; p54tl Digital Vision; p54cr D. Robert & Lorri Franz/CORBIS; p55br Howard Allman; p58tr Picture supplied by Apple, Courtesy of Apple; p58bl Alfred Pasieka/Science Photo Library; p58br Digital Vision; p59t ©2001 Aardman Animations, by Dan Lane; p59mr Screen shots reprinted by permission from Microsoft Corporation; p60-61 (background) Digital Vision

Additional artwork: Andy Burton, Ian Jackson, Kuo Kang Chen, Guy Smith, David Wright, Christyan Fox, Michael Wheatley and Helen Wood.

Additional design, editorial and digital image manipulation contributions: Laura Parker, Keith Newell, Stephanie Jones, Nelupa Hussain, Francesca Allen, Joanne Kirkby, Georgina Hooper, John Russell and Keith Furnival.

Additional consultancy: Stuart Atkinson, Ruth King, Dr. Margaret Rostron, Dr. Kristina Routh, Dr. Tom Weston.